The Brave Little Tailor

A fairy tale by Jacob and Wilhelm Grimm

Retold and illustrated by Bernadette Watts

NORTH-SOUTH BOOKS LONDON

One sunny morning a little tailor was sitting near his window, stitching away happily, when he heard a woman down below in the street, crying, "Good cheap jams! Good jams, very cheap!"

The tailor liked the sound of that! He called, "Come up, my friend! I will buy some jam!" The woman toiled up the stairs with her heavy basket, and the tailor made her unpack all the pots for him.

At last he said, "Your jam seems excellent. Weigh me out four ounces." The woman, who had hoped for a better sale, gave the tailor what he wanted, but went away grumbling.

"God bless this excellent jam!" cried the little tailor. "It will make me healthy and strong." He cut himself a slice of bread and spread it thickly with jam, then put it aside until he had finished his work.

As he stitched away, the sweet smell of the jam attracted some flies. The tailor whisked them away, but they kept coming back. Furiously he pulled a piece of cloth from under his table and swatted them hard. When he looked down, there were seven flies, all dead, with their legs in the air.

"Why! What a brave fellow I am!" said the tailor. "The whole town shall hear of this!" Quickly he stitched himself a belt and embroidered on it in large letters: SEVEN AT ONE STROKE.

The tailor tied on his belt. Before he went out into the world he looked around him to see what was worth taking, but there was only an old cheese, and this he stuffed into his pocket. By his front door he noticed a bird entangled in a bush. He put the bird in his other pocket and then marched proudly along the road.

The road led him to the top of a mountain where a giant sat, resting. The brave little tailor said, "Good day, friend. I see you are looking over the wide world. I am going out there to try my luck. Would you like to come with me?" Contemptuously, the giant growled, "You ragamuffin! You miserable little creature!"

The tailor, with great bravado, displayed his belt to the giant. "You may read there what kind of man I am," he said. Then the giant, believing it was seven men the tailor had killed, felt a little more respect for the fellow. However, to test him, he picked up a stone and squeezed it so that water dripped out. "Child's play!" sneered the tailor, and he pulled the cheese from his pocket and squeezed all the liquid out of it. "That was a bit better. Wasn't it?" he said. The giant was amazed. He picked up another stone and threw it so high that the eye could scarcely follow it.

"Well thrown," said the tailor, "but your stone fell to earth again. I will throw a stone that will never come back." And he took the bird out of his pocket and tossed it into the air. The bird flew away and did not come back. "How about that!" the tailor boasted.

"You can certainly throw," said the giant. "Let's see how much you can carry."
A mighty oak lay felled close by. "Now help me carry this tree out of the
forest," commanded the giant. "Readily," answered the tailor. "You take the
trunk, and I will take the branches."

The giant heaved the trunk onto his shoulder, but the tailor sprang up onto a
branch, so the giant, who could not look round, had to carry both the tree and
the tailor. The tailor whistled merrily as they went along. At last the giant could
no longer bear the weight. "Watch out!" he shouted. "I must let the tree fall!"
The tailor jumped down and seized the branches as if he had been carrying
them, and said, "Can't such a huge fellow as you even carry a tree?"

Further along they passed a cherry tree. The giant pulled down the top of the tree, put it into the tailor's hand, and told him to eat the cherries. But when the giant let go, the tree sprang back and the tailor was tossed into the air. The giant chuckled. "Aren't you strong enough to hold down a twig?" "Indeed I am!" the tailor retaliated. "But I had to leap over the tree because some huntsmen are shooting in this direction. Jump like I did – if you can!" The giant jumped clumsily and got caught up in the branches. So again the tailor won.

The cunning giant invited the little tailor to sleep the night in his cave. So they went together to the giant's cave, and there inside were other giants feasting around a fire. The giant showed the little tailor a bed where he could sleep. The bed was, however, far too big for him, so he crept into a dark corner to sleep. When the giant believed the little tailor to be deep asleep he took a great iron bar and smashed the bed. "That finishes the grasshopper for good!" he said. Next morning the giants trooped off into the forest, having forgotten the tailor. When suddenly he walked up to them, the giants were terrified and rushed away.

The tailor travelled on a long way, until he came to a palace. Feeling weary, he lay down and fell asleep. People saw him and read on his belt: SEVEN AT ONE STROKE. Thinking the tailor to be a great warrior they went to the king and advised him that if war should break out this brave stranger would be very useful to them. A courtier was sent to the tailor to ask if he would serve the king. "That is just why I am here," the tailor answered smartly. The grateful king welcomed him and gave him a fine house to live in.

The king's soldiers, however, disliked the tailor. They said amongst themselves, "If we quarrel with him he will kill seven of us with every blow." So they went to the king and declared, "We do not want to be with a man who kills seven at one stroke."

The king did not wish to lose the loyalty of all his soldiers for the sake of one person, but he was afraid to dismiss the tailor in case he killed him and all his people. After much thought the king said to the tailor: "In the forest nearby live two giants who are dangerous and destructive. If you can kill these giants I will give you half my kingdom, and my daughter as your wife. You may take a hundred horsemen to help you."

"Well, that would be wonderful!" thought the little tailor. "It is not every day one is offered a princess and half a kingdom." He told the king he could easily get rid of the giants single handed. The tailor set out and when he came to the edge of the forest he said to the horsemen following him, "Wait here while I deal with these giants." He soon spotted the giants deep asleep, snoring like thunder, under a tree. The tailor filled his pockets with stones and climbed up the tree to a branch above one of the giants. He started dropping stones down on the giant's chest.

The giant woke up and growled at his comrade, "Why are you knocking me?"
"You are dreaming," growled the other giant. "I am not knocking you." When
the giants fell asleep again the tailor threw stones at the second giant until he
awoke. "Why are you pelting me?" bellowed the giant.

"I am not pelting you!" answered the first giant. Again the giants fell asleep,
and again the tailor threw stones at them. Finally one giant sprang to his feet.
"That's enough!" he roared, and he fell upon the other giant. The two giants
raged like madmen, tore up trees, and beat each other with branches.

At last they both fell down dead. The little tailor leapt down from his tree and
quickly returned to the place where the horsemen were waiting. "I have finished
off those giants!" the valiant little tailor shouted. "It was hard work, but not
too much trouble for a man who can kill seven at one blow." Amazed,
the horsemen did not altogether believe the tailor's story, and they rode into
the forest to see for themselves.

The little tailor claimed his reward, but the crafty king said, "Before you marry my daughter and receive half my kingdom you must capture a fierce unicorn which is causing great damage." "I have no fear of one unicorn," replied the tailor. "Seven at one blow is my style."

The tailor went into the forest, taking a rope and an axe, but leaving the horsemen, who came with him, behind. The tailor soon met the unicorn and the fierce beast ran at him with its horn lowered. The clever tailor stood absolutely still until the unicorn was almost upon him, then he dodged behind a tree. The unicorn plunged its horn so deep into the tree that it could not escape. The tailor fastened the rope round the unicorn's neck and hacked the horn out of the tree with the axe. Then he dragged the beast away.

Still the king would not fulfil his promise.
"You have a third task," he said. "You must
catch a ferocious boar that roams the forest,
causing great havoc." "Child's play!" said
the tailor. The tailor went into the forest alone.
The boar soon saw him and charged at him,
but the tailor raced off.

He ran into a nearby chapel and the boar ran
in after him. But the tailor sprang out of the
window, ran round, and slammed the door.
And so the boar was caught.

And now the king was forced to keep his promise. The tailor received half the kingdom and married the princess with great pomp and splendour.

And that was how a tailor became a king.

One night the young queen heard her husband talk in his sleep: "Boy, stitch that waistcoat, patch those trousers, or I will box your ears!" Next day she told her father her husband was nothing but a tailor and she wanted to be rid of him. The king said, "Leave your bedroom door open tonight, and my servants will hide outside. When your husband is asleep the servants will take him and put him aboard a ship bound for a distant land."

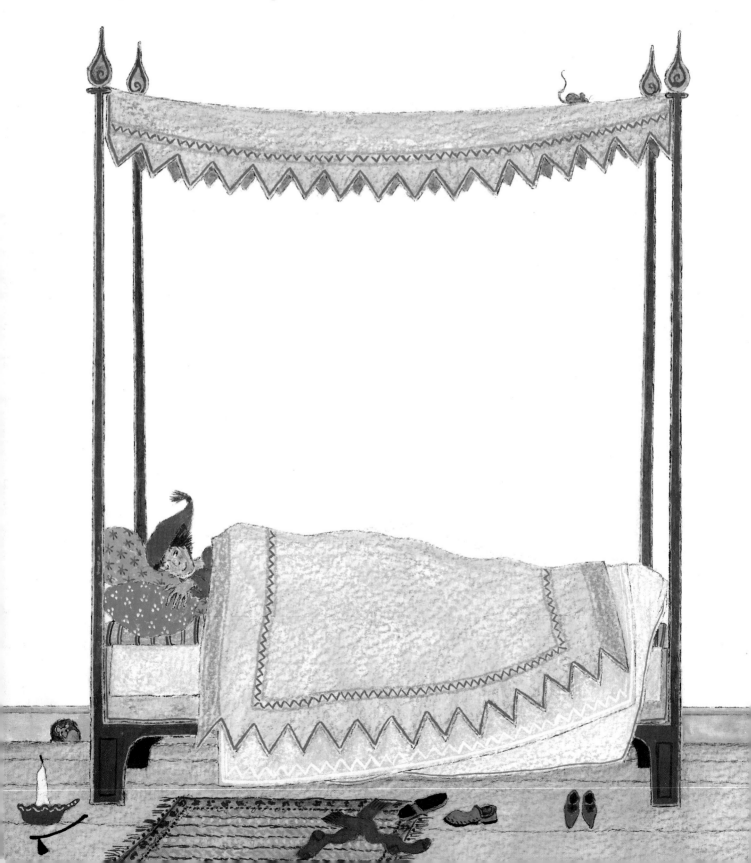

Now the king's armour-bearer overheard the plot and warned the tailor. "I'll soon put a stop to that!" said the tailor. That night he only pretended to be asleep and shouted out, "Boy, stitch that waistcoat, patch those trousers, or I will box your ears. I smote seven at one blow. I killed two giants. I captured a unicorn and a boar. Why should I fear those who hide behind the door?" The servants then fled in terror. Never again did anyone move against him. So the little tailor was a king to the end of his life.

Other books illustrated by Bernadette Watts
and published by North-South Books:

Little Red Riding Hood
Hansel and Gretel
Snow White
Snow White and Rose Red
The Elves and the Shoemaker
The Bremen Town Musicians
Rumpelstiltskin
The Brave Little Tailor
The Snow Queen
Thumbelina
The Fire Tree
Varenka
George's Garden
Tattercoats
The Four Good Friends
The Wind and the Sun
Shoemaker Martin
The Little Donkey
Trouble at Christmas
Fly away, Fly away over the Sea
Goldilocks and the Three Bears

Copyright © 1994 by Nord-Süd Verlag AG, Gossau Zürich, Switzerland
First published in Switzerland under the title *Das tapfere Schneiderlein*
English translation copyright © 1994 by Bernadette Watts

First published in Great Britain, Canada,
Australia and New Zealand in 1994 by North-South Books,
an imprint of Nord-Süd Verlag AG, Gossau Zürich, Switzerland.

ISBN 1 55858 245 2

British Library Cataloguing in Publication Data
is available

1 3 5 7 9 10 8 6 4 2

Printed in Belgium